For Marie-Christine Keith

First published 1984 by
Walker Books Ltd,
17-19 Hanway House,
Hanway Place, London W1P 9DL

© 1984 Nicola Bayley

First printed 1984
Printed and bound by
L.E.G.O., Vicenza, Italy

British Library Cataloguing in Publication Data
Bayley, Nicola
Spider Cat.--(Copycats)
I. Title II. Series
823.914 [J] PZ7

ISBN 0-7445-0155-5

SPIDER CAT

Nicola Bayley

If I were a spider
instead of a cat,

I would scurry
to a sunny corner
of the garden,

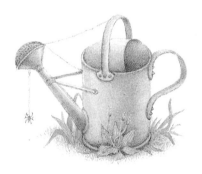

I would spin
the strongest web
in the world,

I would catch flies
and eat them
whenever I wanted,

I would blow
in the wind
on a single thread,

I would see
the whole world
sparkling with dew,

and if ever
I were caught
in the pouring rain,

I would quickly
turn back into
a cat again.